Little Lucy

and the Little Butterflies

Illustrated by Something of a Dandy
SomethingofaDandy.com

LITTLE LUCY AND THE LITTLE BUTTERFLIES

ISBN-13: 978-0-578-70755-6

Printed in the United States of America

Little Lucy

and the Little Butterflies

a story about anxiety

Jordan Corcoran

Illustrated by Something of a Dandy

Griffin.

You are the answer to every question, the reward to every hardship,
and the purpose I have been searching for my entire life.
This is for you.

Most days, Little Lucy
loves going to school.

She loves to learn, write,
and play with her friends.
She loves to ask questions,
be the leader, and enjoy
little delicious snacks.

But for a while now, Little Lucy has been feeling a little worried every morning before she gets on the bus. Her little stomach hurts and she feels like she is going to cry.

Her mom and dad can see Little Lucy is having a hard time, but they don't know what's wrong. They ask her, but Little Lucy feels a little nervous they will be mad, so she doesn't tell her parents how she is feeling.

When Little Lucy stopped raising her little hand during class and didn't want to play at recess, Little Lucy's teacher asked, "Lucy, are you okay? Is there something bothering you?"

Little Lucy felt little butterflies in her little stomach and her little hands started to feel a little sweaty.

She said, "I feel sick. Can you call my mom?"

When Little Lucy's mom came to get her from school,
Little Lucy was a little scared.

Driving home, her mom said to her, "Lucy,
please tell me what is wrong. I want to help."

Little Lucy cried and yelled, "I don't know what is wrong!
I don't feel good, but I don't know why!"

She put her little hands over her little eyes and
cried big tears the whole way home.

LUC

When they got home,
Little Lucy ran to her room,
threw herself on her little bed,
and tried to go to sleep.

Her mom came into the room, and said to Little Lucy, "Sometimes, we feel scared to say how we feel. We think grown-ups may be mad or that we will get in trouble. I want you to know you can come to me, always. No problem is too little."

Little Lucy took a little breath and said to her mom,
"When I wake up, I feel worried about going to school.
My stomach hurts. I want to cry. I don't want to eat breakfast.
I want to hide under my covers. I think about getting answers
wrong in class and that my friends will laugh at me. I don't always
understand what our teacher is saying, and I feel a little sad."

"When I walk to my classroom, my heart starts to beat really fast, my eyes fill up with tears, and I want to go home. I really don't want to feel like this."

Little Lucy covered her little face because she didn't want her mom to be upset with her.

Little Lucy's mom gave her little girl a big hug.
She said, "I know how you feel, sweetie. I feel worried and like there are little butterflies in my stomach. Sometimes I cry and feel like I want to hide under my covers, too."

"You feel that way, too?" asked Little Lucy. Little Lucy felt some of the little butterflies leave her little stomach. She didn't know other people felt this way, too. Knowing that made Little Lucy feel a little better.

Little Lucy's mom then said, "When I feel a little worried and like there are little butterflies in my stomach, I take a really BIG breath and count to 6 while I am breathing in. Then I hold my big breath while counting to 8. Then I breathe out while counting to 4. I do this over and over again until those feelings start to get a little better. Want to try it with me?"

Little Lucy nodded her little head. She would give it a try. Little Lucy's mom took her little hand and, together, they took a big breath in for 6 seconds. They held their breath for 8 seconds, and they breathed out for 4 seconds. Little Lucy let out a little laugh. They did it again. The breathing was helping Little Lucy feel better!

Little Lucy's mom looked at her and said, "I am so sorry you are feeling this way. It is okay to feel a little worried sometimes. When you are at school, I would like you to tell your teacher when you are feeling like that and breathe the way we just did together. Okay?"

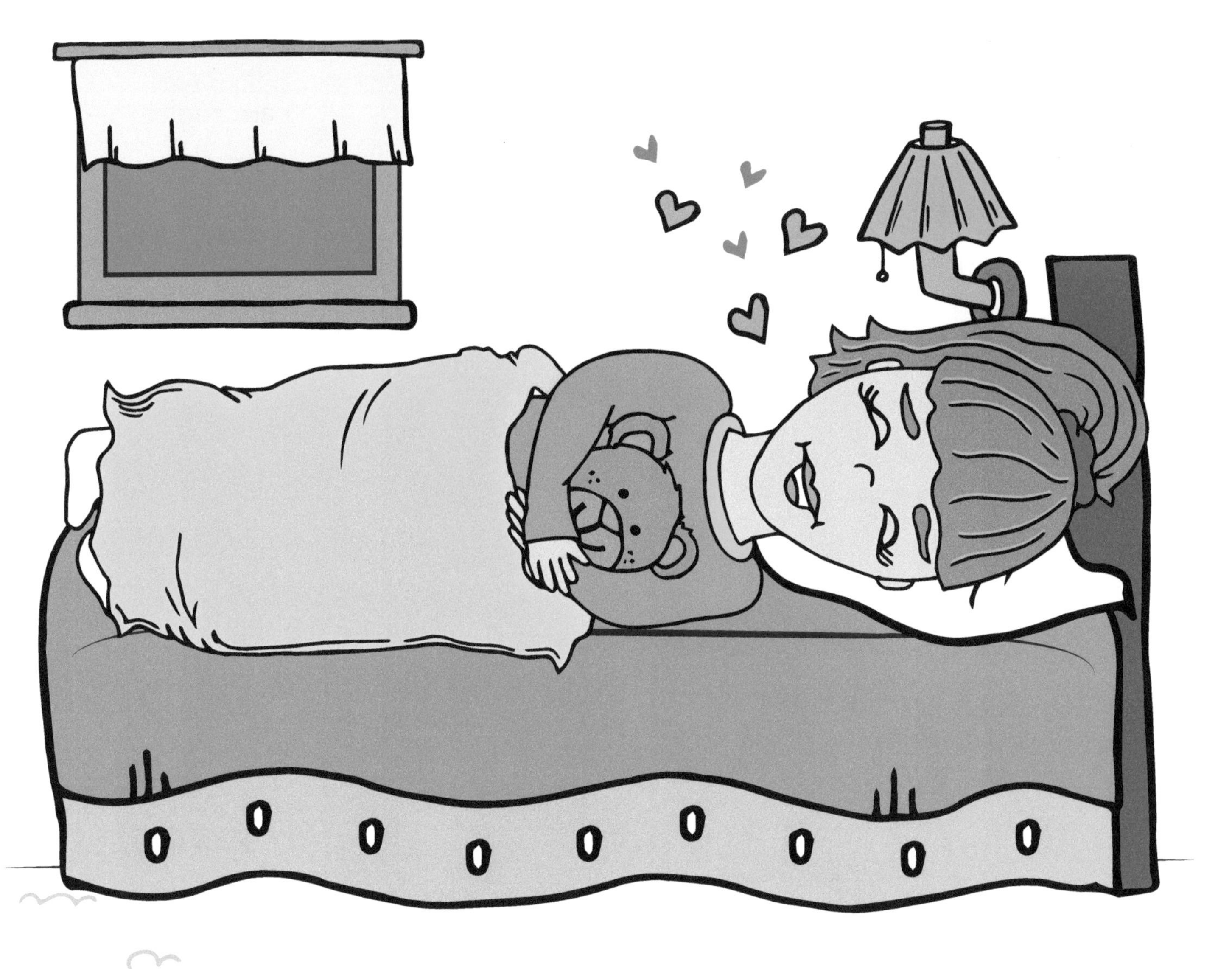

"That sounds like a great plan!"
exclaimed Little Lucy. That night, Little Lucy
went to bed feeling a little better. She hugged her
little bear, closed her little eyes, and drifted to sleep.

The next day, Little Lucy's mom took her into school and talked with her teacher. Little Lucy's teacher told her that she can always come to her when she is feeling a little scared or a little sick. Little Lucy told her teacher her breathing plan, and her teacher thought it was a great idea.

The teacher said she had other ideas, too! She told Little Lucy how she could ask to color, journal, take a little walk, or even talk to the school counselor if her breathing plan didn't work. Little Lucy felt even better knowing that there are many ways to help her feel better.

Throughout the day, when Little Lucy felt those little butterflies or when she was a little nervous to raise her little hand, she did the breathing plan her mom taught her. It seemed to work for a while.

During math class, Little Lucy felt her little stomach do a little flip and her little eyes filled up with big tears again. She was afraid her teacher was going to call on her and she wouldn't know the answer. Little Lucy breathed in for 6 seconds, held her breath for 8 seconds, and breathed out for 4 seconds. She did this over and over again, but the little butterflies weren't going away. Little Lucy started to cry.

Little Lucy's teacher noticed that she was upset. She asked Little Lucy if she would like to go on a walk. Little Lucy gave her teacher a little nod. Little Lucy's teacher and Little Lucy walked down the hall, and they counted out the breaths together and, slowly, it started to work. Little Lucy didn't feel the little butterflies anymore.

When Little Lucy seemed to calm down,
her teacher said to her, "I noticed you got upset
when we started math. Are you having a hard time?"

Little Lucy nodded her little head and said, "I don't always understand what you are teaching, and I am afraid you are going to call on me and I won't know the answer and everyone will laugh at me."

"Oh, Lucy," her teacher said, "we are all learning. You do not need to be embarrassed to ask for help or to get an answer wrong. It is going to be okay. We can work on your math, and if anyone ever laughs at you when you are trying they will get in big trouble. I am so sorry you were feeling this way."

Little Lucy showed a little smile and thanked her teacher. She told her she was ready to go back to class. Her teacher told her to write down the questions she had, to take it easy for this class, and they would go over her questions later on. This made Little Lucy feel relieved.

They went back into class and Little Lucy sat in her little chair and picked up her little pencil. During class, Little Lucy kept up with her breathing plan and also wrote down some questions she had about things she didn't understand.

After class, Little Lucy and her teacher went through the questions and worked through the problems a little slower. This made Little Lucy feel better in a big way. She thanked her teacher for being so great.

After school, Little Lucy got on the bus and, for the first time in a long time, felt happy to tell her mom about her day - even the hard parts.

Little Lucy walked into the house. Her mom had a little snack waiting for her. She sat down at the table and told her mom all about her day, how she felt, how brave she was, and how her teacher helped her.

Little Lucy's mom was so proud.

"Lucy," she said, "it is amazing to me that you worked through your worry with our breathing plan, but when it wasn't working you asked for help and tried something else. I am so proud of you."

Over the next fews weeks, Little Lucy worked through those little butterflies by using her breathing plan, writing down her questions, taking walks when she could, and asking for help. Eventually, Little Lucy started raising her hand more, went back to playing at recess, and even asked to be the leader again. She was so happy that her little smile turned to a big grin, and she started to enjoy going to school again.

RESOURCES

Anxiety & Depression Association of America, ADAA at www.adaa.org

The Balanced Mind Network at www.thebalancedmind.org

Child Mind Institute at www.childmind.org

Child Study Center at www.aboutourkids.org/families

Children's Mental Health Network at www.cmhnetwork.org

Kids Mental Health Information Portal at www.kidsmentalhealth.org

National Institute of Mental Health at www.nimh.nih.gov

About the Author

Jordan Corcoran, Founder of Listen, Lucy

Jordan Corcoran went to Mercyhurst College. During her freshman year, she was diagnosed with Generalized Anxiety Disorder and Panic Disorder. After going through a very difficult struggle with coming to terms and learning to cope with these disorders, Jordan created an outlet where people can openly and candidly share their own challenges and personal struggles.

She speaks publicly to college, high school, and middle school students about her story, Listen, Lucy, and the importance of acceptance - of others and of yourself. She is the author of Listen, Lucy Volume I and Write It Out and has been featured on Today.com as well as UpWorthy.com for her self-love campaigns. Her mission is simple - she wants to create a less judgemental, more accepting world.

CPSIA information can be obtained
at www.ICGtesting.com
Printed in the USA
LVHW071616080920
665352LV00001B/24

* 9 7 8 0 5 7 8 7 0 7 5 5 6 *